To Mitsu and Momo

who helped to make this book

and to Takeo Isonaga

who appears in this story

as a teacher named Isobe

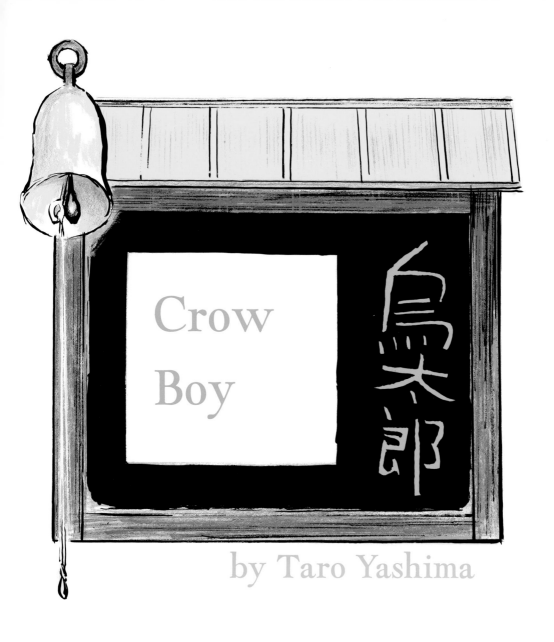

Crow
Boy

鳥太郎

by Taro Yashima

Puffin Books

PUFFIN BOOKS
Published by the Penguin Group,
Penguin Books USA Inc., 375 Hudson Street, New York, New York 10014
Penguin Books Ltd, 27 Wrights Lane, London W8 5TZ England
Penguin Books Australia Ltd, Ringwood, Victoria, Australia
Penguin Books Canada Ltd, 10 Alcorn Avenue, Toronto, Ontario, Canada M4V 3B2
Penguin Books (N.Z.) Ltd, 182–190 Wairau Road, Auckland 10, New Zealand

Penguin Books Ltd, Registered Offices: Harmondsworth, Middlesex, England

First published by The Viking Press 1955
Viking Seafarer Edition published 1969
Reprinted 1971, 1974
Published in Picture Puffins 1976
43 44 45 46 47 48 49 50

ISBN 978-0-14-050172-8
Library of Congress catalog card number: 77-71208
Manufactured in China

Set in Foundry Goudy Modern

Crow Boy

On the first day of our village school in Japan, there was a boy missing.
He was found hidden away in the dark space underneath the schoolhouse

floor. None of us knew him. He was nicknamed Chibi because he was
very small. Chibi means "tiny boy."

This strange boy was afraid of our teacher and could not learn a thing.

He was afraid of the children and could not make friends with them at all.

He was left alone in the study time.

He was left alone in the play time.

He was always at the end of the line, always at the foot of the class, a forlorn little tag-along.

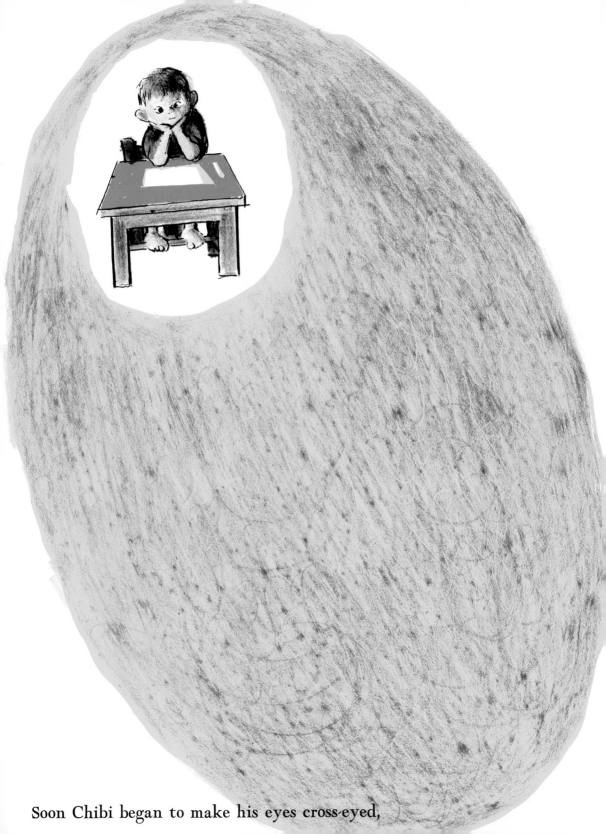

Soon Chibi began to make his eyes cross-eyed,

so that he was able not to see whatever he did not want to see.

And Chibi found many ways, one after another, to kill time and amuse himself.

Just the ceiling was interesting enough for him to watch for hours.

The wooden top of his desk was another thing interesting to watch.

A patch of cloth on a boy's shoulder was something to study.

Of course the window showed him many things all year round.

Even when it was raining the window had surprising things to show him.

On the playground, if he closed his eyes and listened, Chibi could hear many different sounds, near and far.

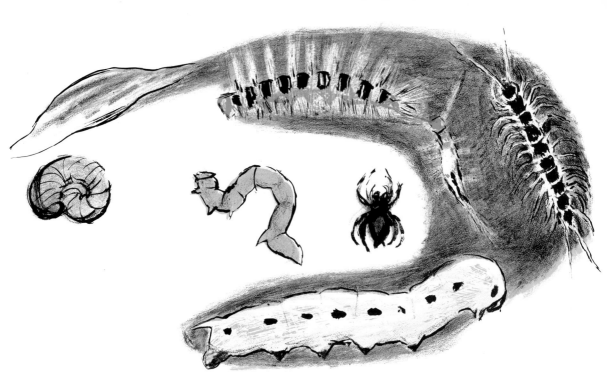

And Chibi could hold and watch insects and grubs that most of us wouldn't touch or even look at —

so that not only the children in our class but the older ones and even the younger ones called him stupid and slowpoke.

But, slowpoke or not, day after day Chibi came trudging to school. He always carried the same lunch, a rice ball wrapped in a radish leaf.

Even when it rained or stormed he still came trudging along, wrapped
in a raincoat made from dried zebra grass.

And so, day by day, five years went by, and we were in the sixth grade, the last class in school.

Our new teacher was Mr. Isobe. He was a friendly man with a kind smile.

Mr. Isobe often took his class to the hilltop behind the school.

He was pleased to learn that Chibi knew all the places where the
wild grapes and wild potatoes grew.

He was amazed to find how much Chibi knew about all the flowers
in our class garden.

He liked Chibi's black-and-white drawings and tacked them up on the wall to be admired.

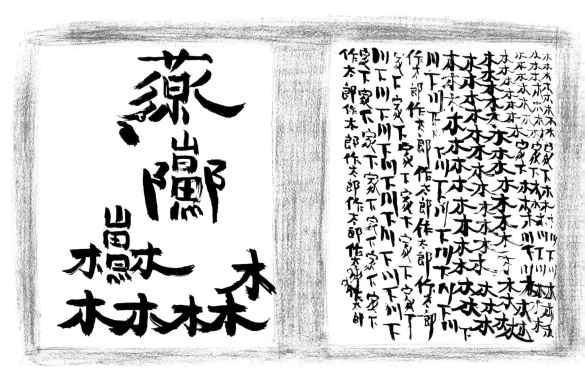

He liked Chibi's own handwriting, which no one but Chibi could read, and he tacked that up on the wall.

And he often spent time talking with Chibi when no one was around.

But, when Chibi appeared on the stage at the talent show of that year, no one could believe his eyes. "Who is that?" "What can that stupid do up there?"

Until Mr. Isobe announced that Chibi was going to imitate the voices of crows. "Voices?" "Voices of crows?" "Voices of *crows!*"

"VOICES
OF CROWS."

First he imitated the voices of newly hatched crows.

And he made the mother crow's voice.

Then he imitated the father crow's voice.

He showed how crows cry early in the morning.

howed how crows cry when the village people have some unhappy accident.

He showed how crows call when they are happy and gay.

Everybody's mind was taken to the far mountainside from which
Chibi probably came to the school.

At the end, to imitate a crow on an old tree, Chibi made very special sounds deep down in his throat. "KAUUWWATT! KAUUWWATT!"

Now everybody could imagine exactly the far and lonely place where Chibi lived with his family.

Then Mr. Isobe explained how Chibi had learned those calls — leaving his home for school at dawn,

and arriving home at sunset,

every day for six long years.

Every one of us cried, thinking how much we had been wrong to Chibi all those long years.

Even grownups wiped their eyes, saying, "Yes, yes, he is wonderful."

Soon after that came graduation day.

Chibi was the only one in our class honored for perfect attendance through all the six years.

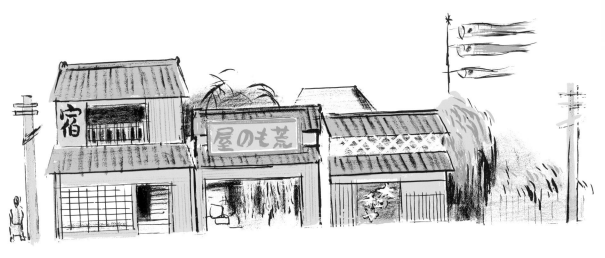

After school was over, the big boys would often have work to do in the village for their families.

Sometimes Chibi came to the village to sell the charcoal he and his family made.

But nobody called him Chibi any more. We all called him Crow Boy. "Hi, Crow Boy!"

Crow Boy would nod and smile as if he liked the name.

And when his work was done he would buy a few things for his family.

Then he would set off for his home on the far side of the mountain,
stretching his growing shoulders proudly like a grown-up man. And
from around the turn of the mountain road would come a crow call —
the happy one.

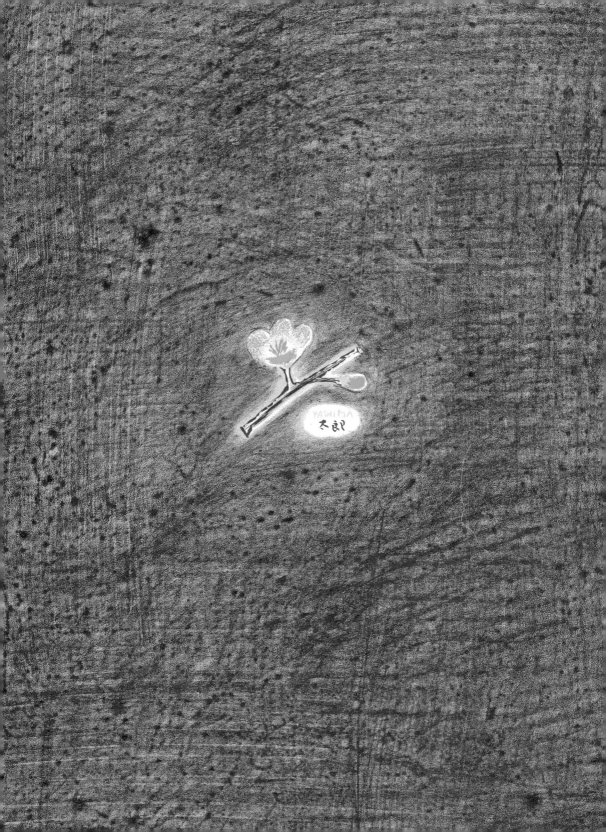